Dear Parents and Educators,

Welcome to Penguin Young Readers! As p[arents] [you] know that each child develops at his or her own pace—in terms of speech, critical thinking, and, o[f course,] [reading.] Penguin [Young] Readers recognizes this fact. As [a result, each Penguin Young Readers] book is assigned a traditional e[asy-to-read grade level] as [well] as a Guided Reading Level (A–P). B[oth of these systems will help you] [choose] the right book for your child. Pl[ease see the back cover for a chart] for specific leveling information [and log on to] [penguin.com/youngreaders] for specific leveling information [by our] esteemed authors and illustrato[rs, classic] [stories,] fascinating nonfiction, and more!

3 4028 09091 7148
HARRIS COUNTY PUBLIC LIBRARY

JER Meiste
Meister, Cari
Tiny goes to the movies

$3.99

DISCARD ocn927378535

Tiny Goes to the Movies

LEVEL **2**

GUIDED READING LEVEL **E**

This book is perfect for a **Progressing Reader** who:
- can figure out unknown words by using picture and context clues;
- can recognize beginning, middle, and ending sounds;
- can make and confirm predictions about what will happen in the text;and
- can distinguish between fiction and nonfiction.

Here are some **activities** you can do during and after reading this book:
- Make Connections: In the story, Tiny and his best friend bring popcorn, a blanket, and a chair to the movie night in the park. If you were going to a movie night, what would you bring?
- Make Predictions: Tiny and his best friend love swimming and playing ball in the summer. What do you think they will do together in the fall?

Remember, sharing the love of reading with a child is the best gift you can give!

—Bonnie Bader, EdM
    Penguin Young Readers program

W9-CON-289

*Penguin Young Readers are leveled by independent reviewers applying the standards developed by Irene Fountas and Gay Su Pinnell in *Matching Books to Readers: Using Leveled Books in Guided Reading*, Heinemann, 1999.

For Jameson—CM

To all the kids through the years in Club 56
who have spent time in our home learning to
love and follow Jesus . . . I am proud of you
and look forward to watching you continue to
grow and be world-changers. I love you—RD

PENGUIN YOUNG READERS
An Imprint of Penguin Random House LLC

Penguin supports copyright. Copyright fuels creativity, encourages diverse voices, promotes free speech,
and creates a vibrant culture. Thank you for buying an authorized edition of this book and
for complying with copyright laws by not reproducing, scanning, or distributing any part of it in
any form without permission. You are supporting writers and allowing Penguin to continue to
publish books for every reader.

Text copyright © 2016 by Cari Meister. Illustrations copyright © 2016 by Richard D. Davis. All rights
reserved. Published by Penguin Young Readers, an imprint of Penguin Random House LLC,
345 Hudson Street, New York, New York 10014. Manufactured in China.

Library of Congress Cataloging-in-Publication Data is available.

ISBN 978-0-448-48295-8 (pbk)   10 9 8 7 6 5 4 3 2 1
ISBN 978-0-448-48296-5 (hc)   10 9 8 7 6 5 4 3 2 1

PENGUIN YOUNG READERS

LEVEL
PROGRESSING
READER
2

TiNY Goes to the Movies

by Cari Meister
illustrated by Rich Davis

Penguin Young Readers
An Imprint of Penguin Random House

I love summer.

So does Tiny.

We like to swim.

We like to play ball.

We like to watch movies.

Tonight is movie night

at the park.

MOVIE in the PARK TONIGHT!

☞ Bring your blanket and **POPcorn!** ☜

I pop popcorn.

Oh no! Too much popcorn!

It is okay.

Tiny cleans up.

Time to go!

I bring the popcorn.

Tiny brings a blanket

and a chair.

We find a good spot.

Tiny is too big.

We have to move.

That is okay.

This spot is better.

Soon it is dark.

Tiny is scared.

I rub his ears.

It is okay, Tiny.

I am here.

The movie starts.

A cat comes on the screen.

Tiny barks.

Tiny barks and barks.

No, Tiny! No barking.

23

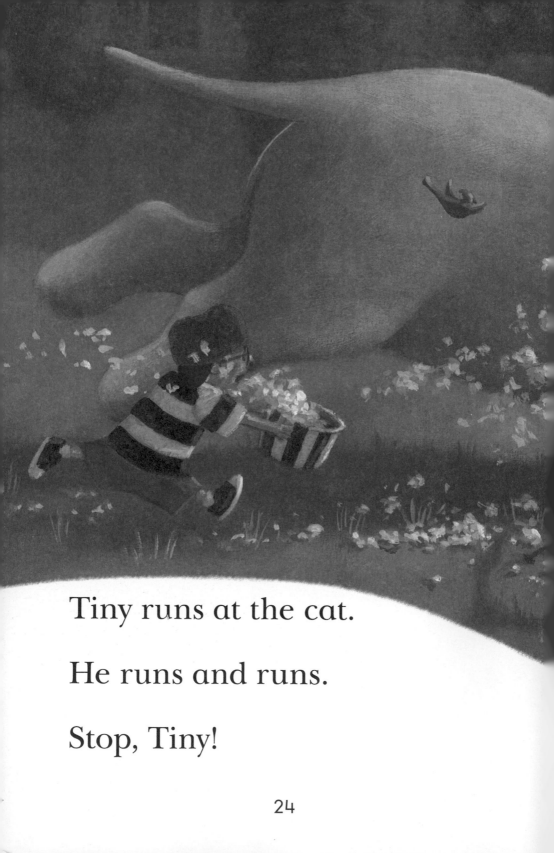

Tiny runs at the cat.

He runs and runs.

Stop, Tiny!

Oh no!

Tiny makes a mess.

He tries to clean up.

They say no.

We go home.

It is okay, Tiny.

Harris County Public Library
Houston, Texas

We can watch a movie

at home!